The Gingerbread Boy

Fairy Tale Classics
STORYBOOK

Once upon a time a sweet old woman had a plan:
"We've never had a child," she told the sweet old man.
"But look—I've found a recipe that we can both enjoy.
It's not a cake; I'm going to bake a Gingerbread Boy!"

She took some sugar, flour and eggs, a pinch of this and that,
Stirred in ginger spice and rolled the dough out flat.
She smiled all the while, because she knew when she was done
She'd have much more than gingerbread—she'd have herself a son!

She picked out five big raisins—three for buttons, two for eyes.
Then she made his nose and smile, cut the perfect shape and size.
She made a wish and opened up the door to her big oven,
Then gave her ginger cookie pan a smooth and gentle shove in.

And while the woman waited in her creaky rocking chair,
Enjoying all the spicy smells that floated through the air,
That oven door flew open and in one ENORMOUS jump
The Gingerbread Boy announced himself, a cookie warm and plump!

The sweet old woman reached for him, crying tears of joy.
She hollered to her husband, "Come and see our boy!"
But the Gingerbread Boy dashed away! Across their fields he ran,
Singing, *"I am the Gingerbread Boy—catch me, if you can!"*

He ran right up to Mrs. Cow, who grazed on grass while sunning.
"Hello-o-o, Gingerbread Boy," she mooed, but he kept right on running.
He sang, *"I ran from the sweet old woman, and the sweet old man,*
I am the Gingerbread Boy—catch me, if you can!"

At Farmer Brown's, the Gingerbread Boy bumped into Mr. Pig,
Who said, "Why don't you stop awhile and join me in a jig?"
But the Gingerbread Boy just ran and sang, a grin upon his face,
So Mr. Pig joined Mrs. Cow and followed in the chase.

Right down to the river's edge, the Gingerbread Boy kept going,
Where Mr. Fox sat in the shade, his hungry eyes both glowing.
"Stop right here," said Mr. Fox. "The river is too wide.
But if you climb upon my back I'll swim you to the other side."

And as they crossed the river, Mr. Fox—who was so sly—
Said, "Climb upon my head. Up here it's nice and dry."
So the Gingerbread Boy climbed up on Mr. Fox's nose of brown,
While Mr. Fox was thinking, "Now I can gobble him right down!"

But the tickle of those cookie feet upon his furry snout
Made Mr. Fox start wheezing and start sneezing all about.
As he sneezed a lucky breeze swept the Gingerbread Boy away,
And the sweet old woman caught him, and took him home to stay!